HARMONY

A VISION FOR OUR FUTURE

Library of Congress Cataloging-in-Publication Data

Charles, Prince of Wales, date.

Harmony : a vision for our future / The Prince of Wales. — 1st ed.

p. cm.

ISBN 978-0-06-173134-1 (trade bdg.)

1. Ecology—Juvenile literature. 2. Nature—Effect of human beings
on—Juvenile literature. 3. Harmony (Philosophy)—Juvenile literature.
4. Environmental responsibility—Juvenile literature. I. Title.

QH541.14C48 2010   577—dc22   2010021957   CIP   AC

Typography by Rachel Zegar

10 11 12 13 14 LPR 10 9 8 7 6 5 4 3 2 1

❖

First Edition

HARMONY

A VISION FOR OUR FUTURE

THE PRINCE OF WALES

HARPER

An Imprint of HarperCollinsPublishers

The Earth

The Earth is a wonderfully magical place.

This beautiful planet, which we call home, is full of life—from the tiniest insect to the largest whale, from the simplest flower to the most majestic rainforest.

The Earth is billions of years old, and millions of people, animals, and plants live here, together. Because there are so many of us, we all need to live together in harmony.

But, unfortunately, humans sometimes forget about the other creatures and plants and damage this necessary balance.

In this book, I want to show you how we can achieve greater harmony among all living creatures.

When we feel ill, our bodies show signs, or symptoms, of our illness, like a runny nose or a fever.

In just the same way, the Earth is beginning to show signs of disease. The ice is melting at both ends of the planet. Animals and plants are disappearing. There is more dust in the atmosphere. You may even have noticed fewer birds in the fields.

These are all signs that something is wrong. So, what went wrong?

There is no simple answer to this question, and different people will give you different answers. What I would say is this: Throughout history, we humans have been brilliant at coming up with new inventions and ideas to make a better life for ourselves. We invented the wheel so we could move things more easily. We built buildings for shelter, work, worship, and learning. We invented medicines to make us better. We created trains, cars, and planes so that we could travel farther and more quickly, and machines to help us provide food, clean water, and electricity for millions of people.

These are all amazing creations, and we all benefit from them. But, while we were making life better for ourselves, we forgot about Nature: the other animals and plants on this Earth where we all live.

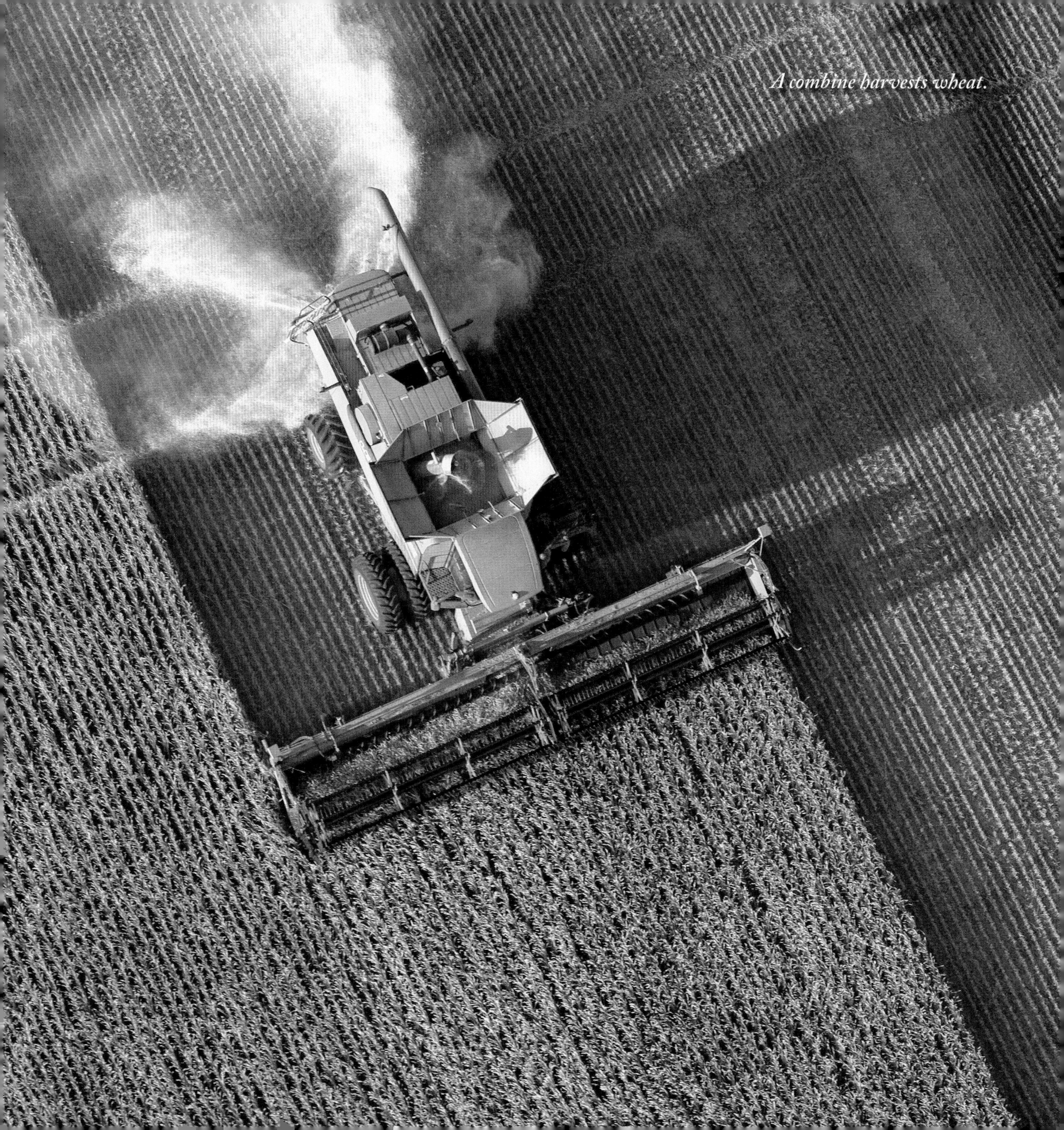

A combine harvests wheat.

Slash–and–burn deforestation

And some very bad things have been happening: Too many chemicals have been used on our farms; large areas of our tropical rainforests have been destroyed; animals have been bred in poor conditions; food often travels long distances; there is far too much pollution, which is warming up the planet, melting the ice, destroying plants, and hurting animals.

If we, and future generations, are to be able to live our lives on this unique planet floating in space, and if Nature is to go on taking care of us, then we must take better care of Nature.

In the rest of this book, we shall see how this can be done.

Lion

Oak tree at sunrise

Planet Earth is home to millions of different plants and animals, each and every one of which is unique. And yet—incredibly—they all link to each other in some way despite these millions of differences.

That might sound strange. For example, what can a lion and an oak tree

Model of DNA molecule   *Heart of a daisy*   *Shell*

possibly have in common?

Actually, they are more alike than we might think because they both contain something called DNA. Tiny DNA molecules exist inside every living thing, rather like a special instruction manual, and are just one of the ways in which Nature is interconnected.

Now let's take a closer look at our DNA molecule. If you look at it under a microscope, it will look a bit like a spiral—in fact, it's like two intertwined spiral staircases, known as a double helix.

Spiral shapes occur many times in Nature. The yellow seeds on a daisy make the spiral shape, as does a seashell and our forefinger when we clench our fists.

Cranesbill flower

Cut apple core

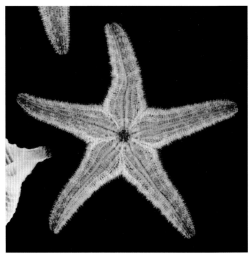

Starfish

Orange slices

The Earth

Water drops

Another shape that occurs many times in Nature is a five-pointed star, such as in the core of an apple when you cut it from the side or in a starfish.

But perhaps the easiest shape to find in Nature is a circle. Before you read on, try to think of as many natural circles, spirals, and stars as you can! I promise you, once you start to look at Nature in terms of shapes, you will begin to see circles, spirals, and stars everywhere!

Do these shapes keep appearing in Nature by chance?

I don't think so! In fact, Nature itself works in a circular way—often called a cycle. We can see this in the pattern of the seasons (spring, summer, fall, and winter), but also in the life cycle of plants and animals.

The more we look at Nature, the more we can see that all the millions of plants and animals have a lot in common. They all connect together.

Bumblebee pollinating marigold flower

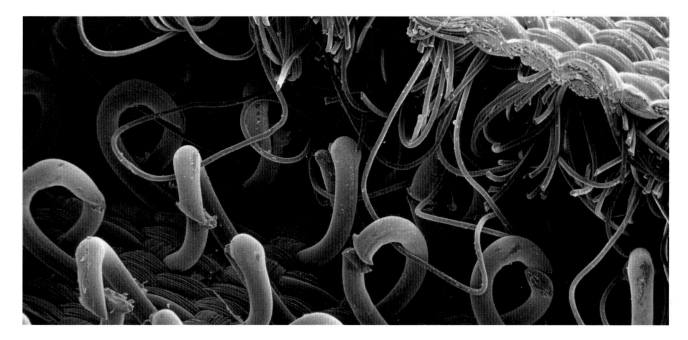

Close-up of a hooks-and-loops fastener

a term that means "to imitate life." One example is the gecko, the small lizard that can walk on vertical walls and even upside down on ceilings. Geckos achieve this remarkable trick with the help of millions of tiny hairs on the underside of their feet. The hairs grab onto even quite smooth surfaces, enabling the geckos to obtain a grip that can easily support their body weight.

Adhesive tapes such as Velcro that use this principle are already being produced and can create extremely strong bonds.

Namib Desert beetle

In the dry and dusty Namib Desert in West Africa, for example, a very clever beetle has found a special way to survive.

Every time misty breezes and thin fogs flow over the desert from the nearby ocean, the beetles go to the top of the sand dunes and turn their bodies to face the wind. The mist settles on tiny bumpy structures on the beetles' backs, where it forms droplets of water that slide down their bodies so the insects can drink.

Scientists have taken this idea to build new structures to collect water in places in the world where there is very little water. This really matters: Throughout the world, millions of people, including children, still don't have access to safe, clean water.

The Namib Desert, Namibia

Fresh mussels

Not all of Nature's clues exist on the land. Some are hidden in the depths of the sea.

Mussels are something that you might like to eat. But mussels also produce a gluelike substance that is stronger than most glues! The mussels produce the "glue" in their fleshy foot and then use this to attach themselves to rocks or other underwater structures. The glue works underwater and is produced at a low temperature, which means that it does not use up much energy. Scientists are confident that we can produce a similar glue for our own use.

Delicious mussels

Lotus flower

When you look more closely, plants also have some amazing secrets. . . .

Lotus plants live in muddy ponds but somehow manage to keep their leaves spotlessly clean and shiny. Engineers studying these plants have found that tiny structures on the leaves stop water droplets from getting a grip. Raindrops are forced to remain blobs that roll, rather than slide, across the leaf. As they roll, they collect the dust particles that lie in their path, so the leaves look clean even after being splashed with mud.

Scientists have taken this idea to develop a new kind of paint, with the same tiny structures. Imagine using this paint on the outside of a building—the building would clean itself!

Office building

The good news is that there are lots of projects all over the world through which people are trying to live more sustainably and more in tune with Nature.

Organic farmers like myself take care to look after the soil: We have stopped using artificial chemicals, and we use different fields for different crops at different times to let the soil recover. We allow our animals to roam freely rather than being penned into buildings like factories. We plant orchards and woods to produce fruit, timber for construction, and wood for energy. We supply local stores and schools so that the things we eat do not have to be transported from different places all over the world.

Most farms do not take this approach because it is still believed that more food can be produced by using chemicals and specializing in one or two crops or animals. But a recent United Nations report, created by many international experts, supported a more traditional, organic approach to farming, and more and more people are now beginning to agree.

The Prince of Wales feeding chickens at his Highgrove home

Children playing

Farming is only one area in which we can, and should, live more in tune with Nature. Another area is our health.

Many children and adults are overweight. Being too big leads to a whole range of health problems and has, I'm afraid, a lot to do with our modern lifestyles. We watch too much television, we play too many computer games, and we don't get enough exercise.

Now here's a thought: Some scientists think that if children spent more time playing outside in parks, they would improve their health and could even do better in school!

Adults who are sick often find that they feel better if they can have access to some kind of Nature—an open window or a bunch of flowers. Many also like to take natural remedies as well as medicine when they are ill.

Again, can we afford to ignore Nature?

Bringing Nature inside

Poundbury, England

Many people know that I am passionate about architecture and the way our surroundings affect us. I care so much about our buildings because where we live is so important in our lives. Lots of us live in cities, far away from the countryside. But this doesn't mean we can't still make Nature a key part of our lives.

We can include local people more in how areas are designed. We can make our homes more environmentally friendly without making them look ugly or like spaceships. We can build more attractive towns where people can walk to work and to school, so they don't have to drive if they don't want to. We can make buildings fit with their natural surroundings and be enjoyable to live and work in. One way to do this is to use the shapes and materials found in Nature.

We live in an amazing world. Nature is all around us. The air we breathe, the water we drink, and the land we live on all belong to Nature. But so do we. Humans are as much a part of Nature as the birds, the oceans, and the trees. To look after ourselves, we need to look after Nature.

And there's still time. If, as some people are doing, we turn to Nature for our inspiration, we might be able to find ways in which we can help preserve our wonderful home for the future. By working in tune with natural harmony and rediscovering much of the abandoned knowledge and wisdom accumulated over countless generations by our ancestors, we might, just might, leave behind a safer, cleaner, and happier world.

I intend to be the Defender of Nature. Will you come and help me?

Prince Charles visits the Harapan Rainforest.

GLOSSARY

Atmosphere— The air or climate in a specific place.

Biomimicry— To imitate life.

DNA— A nucleic acid that carries genetic information.

Earth— The planet we live on.

Gecko— A small lizard.

Harmony— A natural balance.

Life cycle— The natural changes that plants and animals go through.

Lotus— A plant that stays clean in muddy ponds.

Mussels— Shellfish found in fresh water or seawater.

Namib Desert— A desert in West Africa.

Natural remedies— Healing medicine or therapy that uses materials and practices found in Nature.

Nature— The world of living things.

Pollution— The contamination of air, water, or soil by substances that are harmful to living organisms.

Sustainable— Capable of being continued with minimal long-term effect on the environment.

Tropical rainforests— A vegetation class consisting of tall, close-growing trees in areas of high temperature and high rainfall.

PHOTO CREDITS